Quack, Quack, Quack!

Story by Joy Cowley
Illustrations by Jeff Fowler

Norwood Elementary
899 Norwood Drive
West Jefferson OH 43162

Quack, Quack, Quack!
Text copyright © Joy Cowley
Illustrations copyright © Jeff Fowler
Series developed by the Wendy Pye Team.

SUNSHINE™ is a trademark of Wright Group/McGraw-Hill.

Wright Group/McGraw-Hill
19201 120th Avenue NE, Suite 100
Bothell, WA 98011
www.WrightGroup.com

Printed in China through Colorcraft Hong Kong

10

ISBN: 0-7802-4976-3
ISBN: 0-7802-5392-2 (6-pack)

Quack, Quack, Quack!

Story by Joy Cowley

One wet day,
Dad took us to school
in the car.

"Good day for ducks," he said.
"Quack, quack, quack!"

2

3

Dad got out of the car
and took us across the road
to the school gate.

He walked like a duck
and made duck noises.
"Quack, quack, quack!"

5

The next day was wet again.

We said to Mom,
"Will you take us to school?
We don't want to go with Dad.
He embarrasses us."

Then we told Mom
about the duck noises.

Dad came in from the shower.
All he was wearing was a towel.

Mom said to him,
"The children don't want you
to take them to school.
You embarrass them."

"What have I done now?"
said Dad.

"You made duck noises,"
Mom replied.

8

Dad said,
"If I want to make duck noises,
I'll make duck noises!"

He went out the door
and ran around the house,
yelling, "Quack, quack, quack!"

"Quick!" laughed Mom.
"Let's lock the doors!"

We ran through the house,
locking all the doors.

12

13

Dad couldn't get back in.
He stood in his towel in the rain.
"Let me in!"

"No more duck noises," said Mom.

"All right," he said.
"No more duck noises."

15

That morning we went to school
in the car.
Dad grinned.
"Good day for frogs," he said.
"Croak, croak, croak!"

16